Leaving *Mrs Ellis*

Catherine Robinson

Illustrated by Sue Broadley

The Bodley Head

London

Another book for Alexander, with love. *C.R.*

For Becky and Jack. *S.B.*

Child's drawings by Jack Broadley, aged 4

1 3 5 7 9 10 8 6 4 2

Copyright © text Catherine Robinson 1994
Copyright © illustrations Sue Broadley 1994

Catherine Robinson and Sue Broadley have asserted their rights
under the Copyright, Designs and Patents Act, 1988
to be identified as the author and illustrator of this work

First published in the United Kingdom 1994
by The Bodley Head Children's Books
Random House, 20 Vauxhall Bridge Road, London SW1V 2SA

Random House Australia (Pty) Limited
20 Alfred Street, Milsons Point, Sydney,
New South Wales 2061, Australia

Random House New Zealand Limited
18 Poland Road, Glenfield,
Auckland 10, New Zealand

Random House South Africa (Pty) Limited
PO Box 337, Bergvlei 2012, South Africa

Random House UK Limited Reg. No. 954009

A CIP catalogue record for this book is available from the British Library

ISBN 0 370 31856 0

Printed in China

Mrs Ellis was the nicest teacher at Leo's school. She was a kind, gentle lady with a very soft lap. Leo had been in Mrs Ellis's class for a year, but it felt as if he had known her for ever. She was so familiar to Leo, she seemed like part of the family. Not his mum: there was nobody like Mum. But very close. A big sister, maybe. Or an auntie.

Leo often thought he would like to marry Mrs Ellis when he grew up, although deep down he knew he couldn't because she was already married, to Mr Ellis. But he was very fond of her.

Every summer, before all the children went off for their holidays, there was a Summer Fair. This year Leo's mum was in charge of the cake stall, and she had been busy baking cakes and freezing them for weeks.

One day when Leo got home, Mum had all the cakes laid out on the kitchen table. She was icing them, and decorating them; some with tiny coloured sweets, some with hundreds-and-thousands, some with cherries and little silver balls.

Leo's mouth watered. 'Yummy,' he said.

'I thought you could take this one to school tomorrow,' Mum said. 'I thought you could give it to Mrs Ellis.'

Leo was puzzled. 'Why?' he said. 'I thought all the cakes were for the Summer Fair.'

'It's a way of saying thank you,' Mum explained.

Leo was even more puzzled and a bit worried. 'Thank you for what?' he asked.

'Well,' said Mum. 'Thank you for having you in her class this year. Thank you for teaching you so much. Thank you for looking after you. Now, how about testing some of this shortbread?'

But Leo didn't want any shortbread. Suddenly, the cakes didn't look and smell so nice. He didn't want his tea either; he just picked at it. And later, when he went to bed, he couldn't seem to get to sleep.

The next morning, Leo didn't want to get up.

'I want to stay in bed,' he told Mum. 'I'm poorly. I've got a tummy ache.'

Mum felt his forehead, and looked at him. 'Is it a real tummy ache?' she asked him gently. 'Or an I-don't-want-to-go-to-school tummy ache?'

Leo went red, and turned away and looked at the wall. 'It's real,' he whispered, ' I feel sick.'

'Leo,' said Mum. 'Tell me what's wrong.'

Leo turned back again and looked at her. 'It's Mrs Ellis,' he said at last. 'I shan't be in her class any more. Next year, somebody else will be my teacher.'

'But you already knew that,' Mum said. 'Didn't you?'

'I knew in my head,' said Leo. 'I think I did. But it was only yesterday - when you made the cake - that I knew in my tummy. I don't want to leave Mrs Ellis, Mum. I want to stay in her class!'

Mum stroked his hair, and told him that he was growing up, and when you grow up things have to change; otherwise you would stay a baby for ever, and that wouldn't be right.

Leo started to feel a little better. He got up and got dressed, and went to school. But when he was running around the playground with his friend Andrew at playtime, he suddenly thought of something that made him feel ill again. He suddenly remembered who was going to be his teacher next year. It was Miss Lyons.

Everyone was scared of Miss Lyons. All the children at Leo's school were terrified of her. Even some of the teachers seemed frightened by her tallness and her stern face and her loud booming voice. Leo sometimes thought that even the parents must be scared of her.

Miss Lyons' class was always the quietest in the school; Leo thought they must be too scared to make any noise at all. And now he was to be in her class! Leo couldn't bear it.

That night, he had a terrible nightmare. He dreamed he was being chased by an enormous lion with wings like a dragon and a tail like a snake. It was coming for him, nearer and nearer and nearer... He woke up with a jump, hot and sweaty and with a thumping heart. Mum was bending over him, tying up her dressing gown.

'Are you all right?' she said. 'You were calling Mrs Ellis. Was it a bad dream?'

Leo nodded and sat up, wiping the tears from his cheeks. 'It wasn't Mrs Ellis, though,' he told Mum. 'It was Miss Lyons.'

But he wouldn't tell her any more. It seemed so silly, now he was awake. Miss Lyons was just a lady, not a wild animal at all. She couldn't eat him, not really. Could she?

At last, it was the Summer Fair. Leo had mostly been looking forward to it; it was fun, with lots of stalls to spend pocket money, and Throwing the Wet Sponge at teachers, and parents cooking beefburgers, and a Fancy Dress Parade. But part of him was sad too, because after the Summer Fair came the holidays, and after the holidays there would be no more Mrs Ellis.

Mrs Ellis went to the cake stall to thank Leo's mum for the chocolate cake. Leo was there too, helping out and eating all the broken bits.

'It was delicious,' said Mrs Ellis. 'A wonderful cake. It was very kind of you.'

'Well,' said Mum, 'it was from Leo, really. To say Thank You.'

Mrs Ellis smiled. 'He's a good boy,' she said. 'I get very fond of all my children. I miss them all once they've moved up. And I shall miss Leo especially. He paints such good pictures. He painted a lovely picture of a lion last week; it was so good I put it up on display, on the classroom wall. He has a very vivid imagination.'

Leo had heard about vivid imaginations before, from Mum. They were what gave you good ideas for paintings and stories, she said. They were what gave you nasty ideas about horrid things happening, too. They were what gave you terrible nightmares, about lions with dragons' wings and snakes' tails... On the whole, Leo wished his imagination wasn't quite so vivid.

Soon, it was all over. The whole Mrs Ellis year, gone for ever. Leo was very sad to think she would never be his teacher again.

'I know it's sad,' Mum told him, 'but you'll soon get used to it, once you're back at school. Just as you'll soon get used to your new teacher.'

'No I won't,' said Leo gloomily. 'It's Miss Lyons.'

He tried to explain to Mum how horrible and frightening and booming Miss Lyons was, but Mum couldn't seem to understand. All she would say was, 'Try not to worry. I'm sure you'll soon get to like her.'

That night, Leo had the lion-dragon dream again. It was even worse than usual. Afterwards, when Mum had soothed the fear away and gone back to bed, Leo lay awake in the dark. He wondered if he would ever get over leaving Mrs Ellis.

One morning, Mum took Leo shopping with her. She had to go to the supermarket, which Leo usually hated, but Mum had promised to take him out to
lunch afterwards for a treat.

'Can it be pizza?' Leo asked her.

'It can be anything you like,' Mum told him.

So he followed her around the enormous shop, and looked without interest at
packets of biscuits and tins of soup while she filled the trolley. He soon realized
that Mum had stopped and was talking to somebody. It wasn't until he got up
close that he saw, to his horror, that the somebody was Miss Lyons. He couldn't
turn and run; she'd already seen him.

'Why hello, Leo,' she boomed. 'And how are you today?'

Leo didn't answer. He wasn't being rude; he just couldn't speak.

Mum carried on talking to her instead, about Miss Lyons' cats, and while they talked Leo sneaked a look in Miss Lyons' wire basket. Sure enough, there were a lot of tins of cat food. There was also one frozen pork chop, two apples in a plastic bag, and a small jar of coffee. Leo looked at his mother's trolley, and all the food for Mum and Dad and him. He felt a little pang of pity for Miss Lyons and her single pork chop, and just her cats for company.

Miss Lyons was talking to him. 'You paint lovely pictures, don't you Leo?' she was saying. 'I saw your lion painting on Mrs Ellis's classroom wall. Will you paint one for me? Just for fun. Just for me to enjoy. Would you do that for me?'

Leo and Mum looked at each other. Then he looked at Miss Lyons. 'Yes,' he said, in a loud clear voice. 'Yes, I will.'

He started the painting as soon as he got home, but it still took a long time to get it right. It was going to be a picture of cats, as Miss Lyons liked cats, but it didn't turn out like that. It was a picture of his nightmare, the lion-dragon one, but in the picture Leo wasn't running away. In the picture Leo was one of King Arthur's knights, and he was standing over the lion-dragon with his sword held high in the air, because he had fought the monster and killed it, stone dead.

It was a very good painting. Leo thought it was one of the best he had ever done. 'Can we take it to Miss Lyons' house?' he asked Mum, when the painting was dry.

Mum thought about it. 'I think she'd like that,' she said. 'But we should telephone first. Are you sure you wouldn't rather post it?' Miss Lyons had given Mum her address at the supermarket.

'No,' said Leo. 'I want to take it to her.'

So Leo and Mum took the painting round to Miss Lyons' house, which wasn't a house at all but a flat. It was a very nice flat. Leo and Mum sat down while Miss Lyons spread the painting out on her big table, and looked at it very carefully. Leo could hear the slow, gentle tick of a clock.

One of Miss Lyons' cats jumped up onto Leo's lap and spread itself out, purring and pushing at him with its paws. At last Miss Lyons finished looking at the painting. She took off her glasses.

'It's very good,' she said. It was funny, but she didn't seem to be quite so booming any more. 'In fact, it's excellent. And you did it all by yourself?'

Leo nodded. 'It took ages,' he said, and explained the story of the painting, about the knight and the lion-dragon.

Miss Lyons listened carefully to Leo, and when he finished she smiled at him.

Leo had never seen Miss Lyons smile before. It changed her whole face.

'You know,' she said thoughtfully. 'Most people would have run away from that monster. It was very brave of you to face up to it.'

'I know,' said Leo. 'I know that, now.'

'And now,' said Miss Lyons, 'how about some tea?'

There were buttered scones and fruit cake and chocolate biscuits for tea. Leo had orange squash to drink, and Mum and Miss Lyons had tea that smelled like old bonfires. The striped cat sat on Leo's lap again, and Miss Lyons said that his name was Moggy.

'I'm afraid I don't have as much imagination as you,' she told Leo. 'Isn't it funny how we're all here together this afternoon? There's Moggy the cat, there - and you're Leo, the lion - and I'm Miss Lyons! Isn't that strange?'

And Leo had to agree that it was.

On the first day back at school, Leo and his friend Andrew lined up together in the playground. When the bell rang, they went in together. After they had hung up their coats in the cloakroom, Andrew started to go the old way, to Mrs Ellis's classroom.

'Where are you going?' Leo asked him.

'To class,' Andrew said. Then he realized. 'Oh,' he said. 'I forgot. We're not in Mrs Ellis's class any more, are we?'

'No,' said Leo. 'We're bigger now. We're older. We're in Miss Lyons' class this year.'

And off they went, together.